For Rory—may you grow to be a friend
to all animals ~ B. D.

For my loves, Aurelia, Evangeline, Isaac, and Benjamin.
For my other love, James ~ J. P.

tiger tales
5 River Road, Suite 128, Wilton, CT 06897
Published in the United States 2022
Originally published in Great Britain 2022
by Little Tiger Press Ltd.
Text by Becky Davies
Illustrations by Jennie Poh
Text and illustrations copyright © 2022 Little Tiger Press Ltd.
ISBN-13: 978-1-68010-272-7
ISBN-10: 1-68010-272-9
Printed in China
LTP/1400/4075/0821
All rights reserved
2 4 6 8 10 9 7 5 3 1

www.tigertalesbooks.com

The
Last
Tiger

by
Becky Davies

Illustrated by
Jennie Poh

tiger tales

Aasha's forest was once full.

Full of trees. Full of tigers.

Full of life!

Aasha spent her mornings playing hide-and-seek with Koda and her cubs.

And her afternoons
taking long naps in
the banyan tree.

The endless forest sang with
bird calls and the happy
sounds of baby tigers.

But that was before things
began to change.

Sunny days were **hotter.**

And rainy days were **wetter.**

It rained . . .
and **rained** . . .

. . . until one day, there was a huge flood.

To Aasha and the tigers, the forest had become a watery playground. Oh, how they loved to swim!

But the boar had lost their grazing ground,
and soon they left the forest for good.

Aasha was sorry to see
them leave. Boar was her
favorite meal.

She didn't begin to worry until other
animals followed close behind them.
Food was running out!

In the days and months that followed,
Aasha's home changed completely.
Tigers were disappearing.
Some left to find food.
Some vanished without a trace.

And then one morning, Koda
and her cubs were gone, too.

Aasha searched high . . .

and low . . .

. . . but she found only the scent of humans.

Aasha was alone.

Everything was so quiet.

Until, one terrible night, the noises came.

It began with a tap tap tap.

Then a CLuNk-
crash-snap!

And
then
a
ROAR.

Aasha's ears pricked up.
Her nose smelled danger.

Softly, she crept
through the trees . . . .

Huge smoking creatures trampled the forest. Bright silver teeth flashed, and trees fell broken to the ground.

Aasha watched from the undergrowth until daybreak. She watched as her home was destroyed.

Then she turned and ran.

The world suddenly felt very big
for one lonely tiger.

Where would she go?

As Aasha prowled through open ground where trees had once stood tall, she spotted a flash of orange beside her.

Could it be a tiger?

Teman the orangutan peered back at her. Not a tiger.
But he was a part of the forest, and with him close by,
Aasha felt as though she had a friend again.

Farther and farther Aasha traveled,
through a world of unnatural sights
and unnatural noise.

Once clear, the water now ran thick and black.
Even the air tasted different.

Aasha's contact with
Teman became more and
more frequent. It seemed
that he needed a friend,
too. Together, they
felt safe.

After many weeks and many miles, Aasha and Teman came across an untouched path.

Water ran clean and fresh, and on the horizon, they saw earth studded with tiny trees.

This land felt ready for a new
beginning, and so did they.

At last, Aasha found what she was searching for . . .
Hope.
And a new place to call home.

Note from the author

As a passionate animal-lover and dendrophile (tree-lover!), the themes of this book are very close to my heart. I believe that no animal should suffer at the hands of humans—for our food, our clothes, or our lifestyles—and that they deserve to live on this planet as much as we do. But many animals are in trouble. Tigers are just one species that are losing their homes and dying out . . . and once they're gone, we won't ever see them again.

Jennie and I were both incredibly touched by the response of children, parents, schools, and librarians to our first book, *Little Turtle and the Changing Sea*. The awareness of our impact on the natural world is growing so much that there's real hope for the future. Together, we can make a difference!

Glossary of terms

Climate change — The change of the weather on Earth. The weather now is very different from the weather a hundred years ago. Many of these changes are bad for animals and plants, and for us, too—and it's mostly because of humans.

Deforestation — When forests are cut down or destroyed.

Endangered — An animal is endangered when there are so few left alive that they are at risk of disappearing from the world.

Extinct — An animal becomes extinct when there are no more left in the world.

Global warming — A specific type of climate change brought about by humans burning fossil fuels (like coal) and cutting down large areas of forest.

Habitat — A habitat is a place that is home to an animal or plant.

Poaching — The hunting and killing of animals without permission. Poaching is illegal but difficult to enforce.

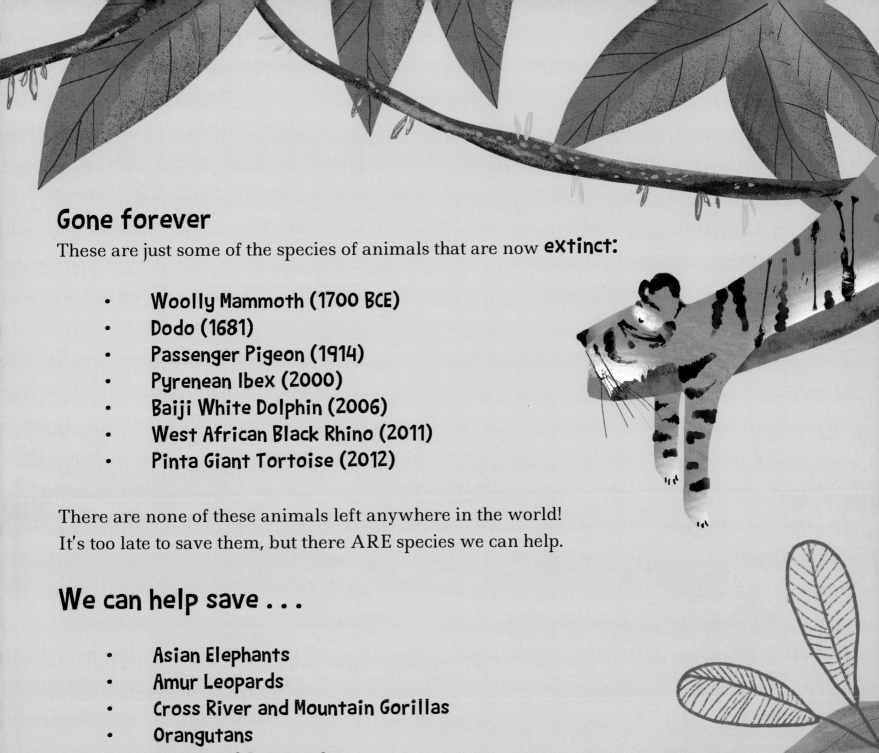

Gone forever

These are just some of the species of animals that are now **extinct**:

- Woolly Mammoth (1700 BCE)
- Dodo (1681)
- Passenger Pigeon (1914)
- Pyrenean Ibex (2000)
- Baiji White Dolphin (2006)
- West African Black Rhino (2011)
- Pinta Giant Tortoise (2012)

There are none of these animals left anywhere in the world!
It's too late to save them, but there ARE species we can help.

We can help save . . .

- Asian Elephants
- Amur Leopards
- Cross River and Mountain Gorillas
- Orangutans
- Green and Sea Turtles
- Sea Lions
- Red Pandas
- Tigers

These species are **endangered**, and humans are mostly
to blame. Many of these animals will experience a similar
story to Aasha, where they see their kind slowly disappearing
around them. If we change our ways, humans can help them survive.

Why are tigers disappearing?

Poaching — Tigers are trapped and killed by humans for their fur, as well as their bones and meat. Some people even believe that tiger body parts can help to cure disease and illness.

Climate change — Increasingly extreme weather conditions around the world are destroying the tiger's natural habitats. This means they're left without a home, clean water to drink, and food to eat.

Loss of habitat — Tigers need space to roam, and they eat a lot! They love deer, wild boar, and buffalo. If a tiger's **habitat** is destroyed, the animals she hunts are gone, too—she won't be able to feed herself or her cubs.

In addition to **climate change**, tigers are losing their homes through **deforestation**. Some forests are cut down to make room for roads or buildings, to make paper, or are cleared for farming—particularly for palm oil.

What's wrong with palm oil?

Palm oil is in everything from pizza and ice cream to shampoo and soap. Rain forests are being destroyed at a dangerous rate due to **deforestation** for palm oil plantations, because we humans use so much of it. It's causing the loss of homes for not only tigers, but orangutans, elephants, and rhinos, too.

Tiger corridors are pathways of hope

Deforestation can mean that tigers (and other wildlife) get stranded all alone in tiny patches of land . . . but that's where tiger corridors can help! They are protected wildlife paths connecting tiger **habitats**, so that tigers can find each other and increase their numbers. Tigers can use them to find new homes— just like Aasha did!

Things are looking up

Charities, governments, and wildlife organizations are working together to protect tiger habitats and stop poachers. And it seems to be working!

Number of tigers in the world:
- 1900: 100,000
- 2010: 3,200
- 2020: Around 3,900

What YOU can do to help tigers and other endangered animals:

- Spread the word and teach your friends what you've learned.
- Make sure that you recycle paper and don't waste this precious resource. Every tree counts!
- Try to reduce the energy your family consumes by turning off lights and appliances when they're not in use.

Further reading

There's a Rang-Tan in my Bedroom, James Sellick and Frann Preston-Gannon, Wren & Rook, 2020

Greta and the Giants, Zoe Tucker and Zoe Persico, Frances Lincoln Children's Books, 2019

Old Enough to Save the Planet, Anna Taylor and Loll Kirby, Magic Cat Publishing, 2020

Online resources:

https://www.worldwildlife.org/species/tiger
http://palmoilscorecard.panda.org
www.wwf.sg/our_work/tigers/